Diary (Almost Cool Witch

Book 1

Meet Cindy – Not a 'Normal' Girl!

Bill Campbell & Kaz Campbell

TABLE OF CONTENTS

Hi I'm Cindy

Squeals and screams shattered the silence of the Math class. Desks and chairs were knocked to the floor as panicking students fled.

My fault...my little spell to create a small black spider to creep out of Poison Ivy's bag (her real name is Ivy, but her personality makes the adding of 'poison' totally acceptable). Well, everything kind of got a little bit out of hand. Instead of one little spider coming out of one bag, I've created hand-sized hideous black spiders climbing out of all the students' bags.

Oh! That extra scream belonged to Mrs. Thompson, our Math teacher.

So make that...*huge hideous black spiders were crawling out of all the students' bags and one teacher's bag.*

I joined the terrified students as everyone stampeded out of the classroom door. We gathered in the garden outside and checked each other's backs and hair for spiders.

It wasn't meant to be like this! I should have listened to Mom when she said, "Witchcraft should only be used when absolutely necessary."

Anyway, my name is Cindy and as you have already realized...I'm a witch. That girl whimpering next to me is my twin sister, Lindy. Lindy is not a witch. Mom is a witch and so is Grandma. But Dad and Lindy are 'normals' – regular humans. As you can guess, that makes our family life both unusual and at times a little difficult.

Even though Lindy and I are twins, we are not identical, in fact, we don't look like each other at all. Lindy looks like Dad with his dark hair and brown eyes and I look like Mom, we share red hair. Sometimes people ask if Lindy is my real sister! I know, it's complicated!

So let me share my diary with you...

The News

Dad came home with a huge smile on his face tonight. Mom looked at him strangely. Normally he was a bit grumpy after school on Mondays...Staff Meeting Days for the teaching staff. You see, Dad is a teacher at my school. I know! It totally sucks having a parent at your own school! But hey, what can I do about it!

Mom asked him, "So why the big grin?"

His smile got even wider. "I have an announcement to make, but I'm going to make you wait a little longer." Mom softly punched him in the arm and shook her head.

So all during our meal, he kept smirking. It was weird! Super weird, in fact! And then when everyone had finished, he went to the fridge and pulled out a bottle of champagne. Mom's eyes widened, you see, Dad is pretty stingy when it comes to money and buying a bottle of champagne is NOT NORMAL for him.

He started by looking at my sister and me, "Girls, do you enjoy sharing the one bedroom?"

What a question to ask, of course we don't! I replied first, "Well, I suppose it is okay if you don't mind being woken up by a snoring hippopotamus every night."

Lindy hit me and replied in a sarcastic tone, "Yeah Dad it's great, especially when SOMEONE keeps wearing your undies because they can't work out which drawers belong to them!"

How dare she accuse me of wearing her underwear, GROSS! "I DO NOT!" I yelled across the table. We both stood up and a war broke out across the dining table. Yelling and screaming at each other until Dad whistled loudly.

"So you girls are saying that sharing a bedroom isn't working, is that right?" he asked.

"Yes, I mean no, I mean..." I tried to explain, tying my tongue into a knot. And then my sister interrupted (she always talks over me), "NO Dad, sharing a bedroom isn't working!"

Dad just smirked and Mom raised her eyebrows.

"I think I have solved our small house problem," Dad smiled and then continued, "I've got some great news."

Mom stood, "Well tell us, what is it?"

Dad was obviously pleased about something. "I've found a way to afford our renovation and build an extra bedroom for the girls."

"Yay!" we cheered. Now everyone at the table was smiling. "I was called into Mr. Janskee's office today and...he offered me a job as an acting Deputy Principal for the rest of the year. "

Mom jumped up and hugged him, she was excited. Lindy and I looked at each other. It was bad enough having a Dad as a teacher at our school, surely he was going to work at a different school... Most of our friends were pretty good about our Dad being a teacher at our school - just, but a Deputy Principal! Dad would make us just behind Sesame Street on the cool list.
I tried to smile, but the frown lines etched deeper and deeper into my forehead. "That's great Dad and what school are you going to be working at?" I asked. I knew this was a silly question, but a girl has to have some hope.

Dad looked at me, "What a silly question Cindy, I'll be working at our school, Paradise Middle School. Don't worry, I wouldn't leave my two girls."

Lindy's head flopped hard onto the table. For a moment I thought she had fainted, but then she started to sob. I personally thought this was a slight over exaggeration of the situation. Please note I said - slight!

"Dad, you are killing me," Lindy sobbed quietly.

Mom and Dad hadn't been taking any notice of Lindy or me for that matter, they were staring into each other's eyes and toasting with their champagne glasses.

Then Lindy stood up and smashed her fist on the table. "You CAN'T be deputy at our school!

And the night continued on like this. Things didn't get any

7

better.

"You're destroying my life!"

"Nobody will want to know me anymore!"

"I'll be an outcast!"

"I may as well move to another country!"

"How can you do this to me, to us!" she screamed.

Dad and Mom looked at me. "How do you feel about it, Cindy?" Dad asked. He had tears in his eyes. I could see the disappointment on his face.

And then there was silence. Cutting and agonizing silence filled the room. It seemed to go on forever. Everyone was staring at me, waiting for my answer.

My mind was like a whirlpool. Should I tell the truth and upset Dad further? Or should I lie and make him feel better?

And then a single solitary tear ran down his cheek.

"Dad if you want the job, I think you should take it," I announced. As the last word came out of my mouth, an apple came flying through the air towards my face.

Lindy had thrown it and unfortunately, she has a pretty good aim. As it was about to hit me, it abruptly stopped an inch from my nose, spun around and returned to the fruit bowl. Thanks, Mom!

Mom looked at Lindy, "Stop it young girl, you are acting like a spoiled brat!"

Lindy gave me a death stare. I was not looking forward to going to our shared bedroom tonight!

"Thank you, Cindy," said Dad in a soft voice. "Lindy, I can understand your feelings, but I promise that nothing will change for you at school."

Once again Lindy's head hit the table - hard. Drama

Queen!!!!

Dad continued, "Besides, it is only a temporary job. Mr. Janskee said if I do really well, then he will consider making me the permanent deputy...but that may not happen."

Lindy's head did not move. We all looked at each other and burst into laughter.

Later that night in our bedroom Lindy refused to talk to me. She only said one word...

I resisted the urge to turn her into a cockroach and instead went to sleep.

She Asked For It!

Lindy is ignoring me...even at school. She refuses to talk to me and pretends she can't even see me. And I'm getting sick of it!

She doesn't even realize how often I have her back. Even today with her being SO RUDE to me, I stopped Poison Ivy from trying to steal the boy she likes.

Ivy was making eyes at Jordy. Giggling at everything he said and flirting like crazy. She kept flicking her long golden perfect hair and blinking her eyes at him. Seriously it was pathetic. Lindy has liked Jordy since kindergarten. It has been a serious long-term crush and over the past term she has actually got up the courage to talk to him.

Poison Ivy went to flick her long hair again and I sent a spell to twirl her hair around the back of her chair. It was classic. Her hair was stuck fast and her fake smile quickly turned to panic. She pulled and pulled, but it wasn't coming free. The more she pulled the tighter her hair wrapped around the chair.

She tried to stand but with the chair hanging from her hair, she could only stoop over. Dragging the chair behind her she struggled out to the teacher's desk. The noise of the dragging chair and the little squeals from Poison Ivy quickly attracted the attention of the rest of the class. The students started to giggle and whisper excitedly to each other.

Miss Burt has a hearing problem...a really big hearing

problem and she stood with her back to the class, neither hearing Poison Ivy's approach or the other students laughing.

For some reason, Poison Ivy quietly whispered, "Miss Burt, please can you help me? My hair is stuck." I don't know why she whispered, the only person in the room who didn't know about her new hair accessory was Miss Burt!

"What? Speak up dear I can't hear you," replied Miss Burt in an extra loud voice...using the volume that people who have hearing problems always seem to use.

Poison Ivy blushed as red as a strawberry as she looked around and realized the whole class was focused on her sudden onset of a terribly bad hair day. The embarrassed Ivy repeated her question louder, which quickly got an instant response from Miss Burt. The teacher sprang from her desk and quickly assessed the situation and then just as quickly returned to her desk and started rummaging around in her desk drawer.

"Turn around!" she commanded in her *oh so loud* voice and Poison Ivy instantly obeyed.

A collective escaped from the watching students as they saw the shiny scissors glittering in her hand.

This was followed by a group gasp...as Miss Burt promptly snipped the large hunk of hair that was wrapped around the chair leg from Poison Ivy's head. Poison Ivy looked shocked as the chair and her hair both fell to the floor.

"Well, back to your desk girl! We can't let a little haircut stop your work."

With sad little sobs, Ivy scooped up her hair and dragged her chair back to her desk. I felt bad, I didn't really mean for that to happen.

But I felt even worse when Ivy came to class the next day with an obviously 'layered' haircut in an attempt make the huge gap in her hair look normal. She had gone from having beautiful level long hair to a very layered haircut. I really should have listened to Mom, magic shouldn't be used for fooling around.

The Magic Apple

Poison Ivy! She was touching Jordy's arm a little too often during assembly and whispering in his ear. Lindy saw this too, her face kept getting redder and redder. And that was when I decided that enough was enough and it was time to put *Love My Sister* into action.

Easy!

Have you ever heard the story about Snow White and the Seven Dwarves? Well, that is where I got my idea from. BUT, the apple wouldn't put Jordy to sleep, it would make him fall madly in love with my sister. Sometimes I even surprise myself with how brilliant I can be.

Step 1 – choose a beautiful red apple.
Step 2 – cast a love spell on it.
Step 3 – get the boy to take a bite.

Simple!

So this is how it all went down...

I chose the reddest of apples, nobody could refuse it!

Then created my own love spell, pretty impressed with that too.

And then the Day Of The Big Bite came along. Jordy was sitting with a group of boys next to our group of girls.

He was telling a story about how he saw a shark in the ocean when he was out surfing on the weekend.

"It was so big and dark, I almost wet myself when I saw it..." He stood up and was mimicking the way it was thrashing in the water. And that was my perfect opportunity to put the apple into his lunch container. Nobody noticed the apple *magically* appear.

"What did you do?" asked one of his friends.

Jordy smiled, "I just ignored it and kept surfing." His friends looked at him as if he was a wild man.

And then he continued, "Nah, I paddled so fast to shore that I think I broke a sea to land record!" They all laughed.

He looked down. Saw the apple. Picked it up and took a bite. Perfect!!! Nothing seemed to happen. He looked perfectly normal. "This apple is the best I've ever had," he commented.
I smiled, happy with my creation.

One of the other boys asked, "Can I have a bite?" It was Will. Cindy and I call him – Wild Willy because he has really wild hair.

Jordy looked at him for a few seconds and then threw the apple to Will.

Before I could do anything, he took a bite. A big juicy bite! "NO!" I wanted to scream, but it was too late.

Wild Willy had a huge smile on his face, "Wow, this is the BEST apple ever!"

The consequences were whirling around my head. What if the spell works?

Then Lochie grabbed the apple and also took a bite. "Yeah man, I have to agree, 100% best apple ever!" At least Lochie didn't look like he's been standing behind a jet engine about to take off. He was pretty good looking, but a little too cool for school...if you know what I mean.

The boys raving on about the magnificent apple...caught the attention of everyone in our group.

I haven't told you about Cate yet. She is a *'kind of'* friend. To be honest, she is pretty painful. You see Lindy and I call her Copy Cat Cate. Yep, one of those people who can't be original. You buy a new top. Oh look, Copy Cat Cate has the same one. She even copied the school backpacks Mom bought us this year.

Getting back to what happened next...

Copy Cat Cate called out, "Hey Lochie, can I have a bite too?"

Lochie threw the apple to Cate and she took a bite. Now, this was getting way out of control. I had to stop it before the whole school fell in love with Lindy.

"My turn!' I yelled, in a voice that sounded a lot like my mother's when she wants the dishwasher packed. Cate threw the apple towards me. My hand was reaching out...and Poison Ivy came from nowhere and swiped the apple and took a bite.

"NOOOOOO!" I screamed. "GIVE IT TO ME!" And I yanked the apple from her grasp.

Everyone was shocked by my over-the-top reaction. Lindy grabbed my spare hand and pulled me down onto the seat. She whispered, "It's okay Cindy, it's only an apple."

Have you ever heard the expression – *Saved By The Bell*! Well, that is what happened. The bell to end lunch rang and everyone quickly packed up their gear and headed back towards class. I still had the apple in my hand, it had 5 bites in it. Checking that nobody was looking, I tossed it into the garden under a bush and tried to act like a normal 12-year-old girl.

But when we returned to class...nothing was normal!

Lochie, who had no manners what-so-ever, was holding the door open for Lindy. "After you Lindy," he said. "My, your hair looks beautiful today." Lindy looked at him and laughed, then her hands moved to her hair, fearing that something was on it.

Lindy and I usually sit together in class. Lindy on the left and me on the right. But when I went to sit down, Copy Cat Cate had beaten me to my seat. "I want to sit next to Lindy," she announced, with a determined *I'm NOT moving* look on her face.

Lindy looked at me and shrugged, raising her right eyebrow. I sat behind them to see what was going to happen. Poison Ivy sat next to me. She gave me a dirty look and said, "Why can't you be more like your lovely sister?"

Copy Cat Cate sat there gazing at Lindy. "I want to be just like you Lindy," she gushed.

Ivy was hanging on every word. "So do I, Lindy, my greatest dream would be to have you as a sister, we could hang out 24/7!"

Turning around, Copy Cat Cate sneered at Poison Ivy. It was almost cat like...sly and threatening. Then Cate turned her back on us and stared at Lindy again.

I could hear Lindy trying to tell Cate that she should be her own person. She didn't need to be like her or copy her in any way because if she searched hard enough, she would discover that she could be her own person.

But the words didn't seem to penetrate Cate's thick skull.

Our teacher, Mrs. Thompson, announced, "Class, for our

next activity I'd like you to form groups of three." Within a second, Cate, Ivy, Jordy, Will, and Lochie were beside Lindy. All five of them demanding that Lindy HAD to be in their group. They were fighting over her. Yes, actually shoving each other out of the way.

Will pushed Jordy over. "She's mine!" he yelled.

"Choose me Lindy!" yelled Lochie. His coolness had disappeared.

Jordy stood up and told the rest of them, "You all know I love her, so go away!"

Lindy looked shocked, but when Jordy said the 'L' word, I could see her heart fluttering.

Of course, Copy Cat Cate came in with, "I love her too, so

you go away." Even in an argument, she couldn't come up with her own thoughts and words!

And Poison Ivy was her usual mean self. "Why would you hang with any of these losers? Lindy, I'm the only one at your level of coolness."
All five of them were pushing forward, shouldering each other and trying to get as close to Lindy as possible. And then the fight broke out. Will pushed Jordy again. This time Jordy stayed on his feet and pushed back and in the next second, they were rolling on the floor wrestling each other. "She's mine!" "NO, she's mine!"

Mrs. Thompson ran over and told them to stop. Both were sent to the office to explain to the Principal why they were fighting in the classroom. I would have loved to listen to that explanation.

So in the end, Cate and Will got to join Lindy in a group. Lucky Lindy! While I was in a group with Ivy. Lucky me!!! Jordy and Lochie joined our group when they returned from the Principal's office...still shoving each other.

This was definitely not my lucky day. Those two boys couldn't concentrate on our task, they had big sad moon eyes and watched Lindy constantly. And Ivy sat there with her arms folded, sulking because she had missed out on working with Lindy. I had to do all the work!

"All right you three, enough is enough!" I demanded.

Jordy just ignored me. Ivy raised her eyebrows and sighed. At least Lochie replied, "What?" Mind you, when he said this one word, he still didn't look at me, his eyes were glued to Lindy.

I looked over and Cate was giving Lindy a neck massage, while Will was doing all the work and looking up at his beloved Lindy every few seconds. She was having a ball!

I looked at Jordy. "Earth to Jordy...Earth to Jordy...please come-in Jordy," I said sounding like a robot.

Jordy replied, "What is it now Cindy, can't you see that I'm concentrating."

"On what?" I shot back.

He looked flustered, not sure what to say.

"So Jordy, be honest, how do you feel about my twin sister?" I asked.

"She's amazing, so beautiful and talented and smart. I love her."

I smirked, wow that spell must have been really powerful. Time to reverse it on those totally obsessed kids.

First I focused on Will and I could tell the second it wore off. He dropped the pen he was holding and complained, "Lindy, stop being so lazy. I've done all the work and I'm not writing another word!"

Next was Copy Cat Cate. There is another personality problem with Cate, she can't accept responsibility and whines like a cat howling at the moon. "I'm not doing it and you can rub your own neck if it is sore Lindy." Yep, back to 'it's all about me' Cate.

Lochie was next. He flicked his hair and shook his head (ever so cooly) like he was shaking off a bad dream.

Poison Ivy flicked her hair and commented, "How did I end up in a group with you Cindy? At least Jordy is in the group."

Now Jordy was the only one left and being the great (I should say – absolutely wonderful sister) I am, I left the spell on him.

After class on our way home, Lindy told me about her weird afternoon. "It was as though Cate and Will had taken some happy pills. They were so nice to me and all of a sudden they turned back into their old sourpuss ways.

I smiled at her, "That is so weird." Lindy hadn't twigged that it was a magic love apple that had caused their sudden and abrupt change of behavior.

Love Is In The Air

The next day at school Jordy hung around Lindy like a bee after honey. He was buzzing around her non-stop!

He held the door open for her...what 12-year-old does that?
Sat next to her in class.
Sharpened her color pencils...really???
Picked up some paper she accidentally dropped on the floor.
Nudged her when she wrote down an incorrect answer and showed her his correct one...wish he did that for me!
Asked if he could join her at lunch.
Sat really close to her...and I mean really really close!
Opened his lunch box and gave her a small flower.
Offered to share his muffin.
Laughed and smiled at EVERYTHING she said.
And sat there, the whole day, staring at her with dreamy eyes.

Of course, this was everything that Lindy had ever hoped for! But she was getting suspicious. REALLY suspicious!

When the bell rang for school to finish, he stood and held her hand and helped her up. Maybe the spell was a little too strong.

"Lindy, will you be my girlfriend?" Jordy asked, in front of the whole class.

Lindy was shocked but very happy at the same time.

"Sure Jordy, that would be cool," she replied. Everyone burst into loud cheers.

Jordy pulled out a friendship ring and asked if he could put it on her finger.

It was almost like an engagement; like he was asking her to marry him!!!!

Now I was worried. What if he didn't actually like her. Had I let it go too far? Was it right to keep him under the love spell? Would Lindy get hurt? Should I stop the spell now? Or keep it going? All these thoughts were whirling through my brain.

On the way home, Lindy didn't stop smiling and looking at her ring. "I can't believe it, Cindy! I can't believe that he finally likes me. I'm so happy!!! And look at this ring, it is the prettiest ring I have ever seen."

Guilt hit me! What had I done?

Guess Who's Coming to Dinner

Okay, I know Dad needs to suck up to the Principal. He wants that job! But, does he have to invite him to dinner...in our house! Of course, we all got the lecture about using our manners and being on our best behavior.

"Seriously Mom and Dad, you don't need to remind us how to be humans," I said, hoping they would calm down. Mom gave me a tense smile and winked. Dad continued on with his list of rules.

"And finally, make sure you excuse yourself from the table when we have all finished eating," he said seriously.

Finally, Mom spoke up, "That's a little over the top."

He shook his head. Dad was obviously stressed about the whole dinner thing.

Luckily the phone started ringing at that precise moment. It was Grandma. Mom took the phone and walked into another room, the conversation was in quiet tones.

Just as Dad had settled down and was reading a news story on his laptop, Mom came in with some news of her own.

"I've got some great news, my mother is coming to stay with us for a few days," she said with a half smile on her face.

Dad doesn't really like Grandma very much. You see in our family we have a number of people who are a little different and Grandma is one of those *different* people. Well, so am I...and so is Mom...we are all witches. But Dad and Lindy are 'normals' and that is how Dad would like us all to be.

"When is she coming?" Dad asked.

Mom tried to make light of the news, "She's got a few days spare, and she is really missing all of us, so she is coming tomorrow afternoon. Isn't that great, we haven't seen her for at least a month."

Dad's face turned beetroot red, "TOMORROW AFTERNOON! She can't come then, my boss is coming around tomorrow night!"

Lindy and I looked at each other and quietly snuck away to our room. But we could still hear every word, and Dad was definitely NOT happy.

"You know she is certified CRAZY! She'll ruin everything for me! Make her come the day after!"

And then he said something that tipped Mom over the edge. "Why did I have to marry a witch?" That was not cool Dad! It also hurt my feelings. Lindy came to me and gave me a big hug.

Mom didn't say a word, but we heard the front door slam.

Just A Normal Dinner Party – NOT

Okay, here's how it worked out. They are both coming to dinner. Yes, Grandma and the Principal. It's great because Dad is no longer worried about our manners! Yes, he has much bigger things to worry about.

The whole family cleaned the house. Why is it that when you know someone is coming over, parents turn into Army generals and demand that every inch of the house is scrubbed shiny clean?

There are some positives though. I always blame Cindy for using my undies. They keep disappearing. And after cleaning my room, I know where they are disappearing to...under my bed. I found 7 pairs! Had to sneak them out from under there! I stuffed them under my shirt so Lindy didn't see, then I casually strolled to the laundry and put them in the washing basket.

Dad decided on a BBQ dinner. I think he wants to be able to get Mr. Janskee outside, away from Grandma...just in case she goes into 'witchy' mode. And Mom is making one of her famous pavlovas for dessert.

Of course, if Mom wanted to, she could use magic to get the housework and cooking done. But Dad doesn't like her doing that and most of the time she lives like a normal.

Grandma, on the other hand, doesn't believe in wasting her time doing mundane jobs, she uses her magical powers to get everything done. And I think I want to be more like Grandma, especially when it comes to cleaning my bedroom and doing homework!

Grandma arrived in the mid afternoon. She looks great for her age (I think she is about 60) and always dresses immaculately. We actually heard her before we saw her. Grandma is a pretty loud person. She ran into the house and kissed my Mom, waved at my Dad and gave Lindy and me the biggest bear hugs before kissing us all over the face, leaving red lip marks. This is her idea of a joke, which was funny when we were 5 years-old...not so much now.

I looked over at Dad, his right eye was twitching. "Thelma, do you really have to stain their faces every time you see them?" he asked.

Good one Dad, get on her bad side from the very first moment.

Dad opened his mouth to continue, but no sound came out. Well, not a human sound. He was talking in pig noises. His eyes opened wide and he looked at our mother. He was definitely very angry!

Mom was trying not to smile. She looked over at Grandma and said, "Come on, that's just being mean, although he was mean to you first, he doesn't deserve to sound like a pig."

Grandma shrugged her shoulders and pointed at Dad.

Mom did say he didn't deserve to sound like a pig...and I suppose Grandma did make a change. But now Dad was sounding like a goose honking.

His face was really angry now, turning a deeper shade of red by the second.

"So Bruce, now we've had our family fun, I'm going to return your voice, but make sure it stays civil," Grandma warned.

Dad knew when he was beaten. He quietly apologized to Grandma (he said one word – sorry) and left the room. With his boss coming for a BBQ tonight, the last thing he needed was to sound like a pig or a goose!

Cindy and I went upstairs to help Grandma unpack. As we walked into her room, the clothes from her suitcase were flying around the room, organizing themselves into colors and then landing on the coat hangers in the wardrobe. There was no doubting that our Grandma was pretty different and very cool.

Telling stories of her adventures is Grandma's specialty. She told us of her latest travels around the world, including visiting the Egyptian Mummies and a haunted house in London.

While she was finishing off the story about a ghost, our mother walked in.

"You're not telling that old story again?" she asked, smiling. Obviously, Mom had heard the story before. Grandma laughed and finished the story. We clapped and cheered! There was nobody like our grandmother.

Mom sat down on the bed with us. She held Grandma's hands and looked into her eyes with a serious gaze. "Mom, I'm so happy you are here, I've missed you so much. But I have to ask you to do something for me."

Grandma's forehead creased, "Is everything okay sweetheart?" she asked.

"Everything is great, in fact, Bruce has had a job promotion at school," Mom said, obviously proud.

Grandma hugged Mom, "Don't tell me he is finally the Principal of that little school?"

Mom looked shocked, she didn't know what to say. I helped her out. "No Grandma, he is an acting Deputy Principal for the rest of the year. We'll be able to afford to make our house bigger so that Cindy and I can have our own bedrooms."

"Acting...did you say *acting Deputy Principal*?" she said

sarcastically.

Mom's jaw dropped. "Yes she did say acting and deputy...and I couldn't be more proud of him. And tonight is very important to him. His boss, Mr. Janskee, is coming around for a BBQ and Bruce wants to make a good impression. So for tonight, we are no longer witches, we are normals! No witchcraft, no sarcastic comments, and no arguing! Mom, you have to agree to be on your best behavior and not embarrass Bruce."

With glistening eyes, Grandma looked a little hurt. "Of course sweetheart, I can see that this is very important to you. Don't worry, I'll be on my best behavior," promised Grandma. She gave Mom a reassuring cuddle.

***

Okay, I won't bore you with the details, just the juicy parts!

First up...Grandma and Dad's boss, Mr. Janskee, are from two different universes. You know what I mean – total absolute opposites!

Grandma is warm, happy, outgoing and positive.

While Mr. Janskee is boring, dull, negative and serious.

So even before the night began, it was obvious that it was going to be a clashing of two worlds. Oh, I forgot to mention, they are both single. Mom reckons it would take a SUPER person to cope with either of them!

***

The doorbell rang on the very second that Mr. Janskee was

due to arrive. This was taking punctuality to the extreme!
Our dog, a cute little Pomeranian called Fluffy was the first
to the door to greet him.

Wagging his cute little bushy tail, Fluffy was thrilled to meet
someone new. And to my surprise, Mr. Janskee picked him
up and gave him a huge cuddle and tummy rub. *Could this
man actually have some feelings? Could he actually be nice...*and
then I decided that he was a dog person and I imagined him
living with 30 or so dogs in a dark and smelly apartment.

Everyone greeted him, including Grandma and we all
moved to the back deck. Grandma was on her best behavior
and I could see Dad's concerns slowly fading.

Mom dished up dinner...barbequed meat, spaghetti
bolognese, salads and garlic bread. It certainly was a feast.

Mr. Janskee helped himself to everything and Grandma made a comment that sounded weird. She said, "I love a man with a good appetite." Then she winked at him. Lindy kicked my leg under the table and Mom and Dad smirked at each other. But Grandma and Dad's boss didn't seem to notice our reaction.

The spaghetti was really long and Mr. Janskee was having trouble picking it up with his fork. A long piece coated with tomato sauce flicked against his cheek, leaving a red streak across his face.

Lindy and I started to giggle. But almost as soon as we had started, our giggling stopped and our lips were sealed shut. The red sauce on his face lifted and flew back into his bowl. Grandma winked at us and suddenly we could open our mouths again.

He put his fork into the spaghetti again. Wouldn't most people just leave it! But I do have to admit...Mom's spaghetti is world class. As soon as his fork hits the pasta, it wrapped neatly around his fork. Mr. Janskee stared at the fork and his mouth fell wide open.

"How did that happen?" he blurted out. Mom had seen it and quickly said, "Oh Kevin, we bought these forks in China last year when we were on vacation. Aren't they amazing?"

Mr. Janskee (I can't bring myself to call him Kevin) shook his head, "They are amazing Hazel, I'll have to order some for my home."

Finally, Dad twigged that there was magic at play and he quickly changed the subject. "Kevin, we have a little game we play with new visitors, it is called three questions and we have to try to guess your answers, want to play?" Dad asked.

Looking a bit puzzled and maybe slightly anxious, Mr. Janskee replied, "Ahh, yeah, sure."

Dad smiled, but beneath the smile, I could see stress. "Okay first question, where is your favorite place to take holidays?"

Smiling, he replied, "You'll never guess that answer."

"Hawaii!" yelled Lindy.

I called out, "New York!" But he shook his head.

Mom guessed London, but she was wrong too.

Dad tried Canada...wrong.

Grandma was the last to have her turn. "Paris," she said quietly.

"How did you know that?" Mr. Janskee was astonished that she had guessed correctly.

Fluttering her eyelashes, she said, "I can tell that you are a romantic and sensitive man, so I chose the city of love."

Absolute silence! It was as if the room has been frozen still. Nobody moved, nobody made a sound. Was my Grandma flirting with my school Principal?

A smile slowly formed on Mr. Janskee's face, "That is the nicest thing anybody has ever said to me, thank you, Thelma, you have made my night very special." They were staring into each other's eyes.

I wanted to vomit! I wanted to scream NO! Dad started choking on his food and Mom hit him on the back.

When Dad settled down, he asked the second question. "So Kevin, what is your favorite food?"

Once again all our guesses were wrong. Until it came to Grandma's turn. "I think you like pavlova," she said, her eyes twinkling.

This time he pushed his chair back and stood up, obviously excited. "You are incredible Thelma! How did you know that?" he asked.

Yeah, how did she know that!!!!

Grandma coyly rolled her eyes and lowered her chin, "A sweet man like you Kevin, would like a sweet dessert and that is why I chose pavlova."

I couldn't help it...I started to laugh. Mom reached over and pinched me on the leg and gave me a stern look.

Dad rushed onto the third question. I could see that his brain was desperately searching for a straightforward question that Grandma couldn't manipulate. "I love pavlova too Kevin, in fact, we are having my wife's famous pav for dessert. Now for the third and final question...what is your favorite color?"

I guessed first, "Black." This time Dad kicked me under the

table. By the end of the night, I was definitely going to have several bruises!

Lindy guessed brown. I knew her thinking, she saw him as a dull person and thought brown suited his personality.

Red was Dad's guess and Mom suggested green. But once again, we were all wrong.

Grandma smiled, "Kevvy, you don't mind me calling you Kevvy?" "Is your favorite color orange?" she asked.

We all waited with bated breath. Could she be right again?

Kevvy baby smiled, "Well Thelma, that is my second favorite color, but my favorite is blue."

We continued to eat and then Grandma walked back into the kitchen to get some orange juice from the refrigerator. When she returned, she was wearing a blue dress, blue shoes and had blue fingernail polish on.

Dad freaked! He didn't say anything, but the look on his face was just like the people who go into hot dog eating competitions, just before they vomit up a disgusting mess of bread and sausages.

Trying to attract Grandma's attention, Mom was making hand signals for her to stop it.

And then Mr. Janskee looked up. He was obviously shocked and it took him a moment to regain his composure. "Why Thelma, that was a quick change and can I say you look absolutely beautiful in blue."

With a scrape of her chair, Mom stood and asked Grandma to help her with dessert in the kitchen. I don't know exactly what was said, but when they returned with the pavlova and new plates, Grandma seemed a little (and I said a LITTLE) less flirty.

Just as Mom put her perfect pavlova onto the table and everyone was complementing her...it went down. It gradually lowered until it was as flat as a pancake.

Horrified, Mom, started to apologize, "I'm so sorry, this has never happened to me before."

Before our eyes, it started to rise again. It got bigger and bigger until it returned to its normal size.

But it didn't stop there, it continued to grow and grow until it was almost at our eye level. Grandma was obviously at work again.

Then it started to go down again. However this time it stopped at its normal height. Mom's magic had brought it back to normal.

But no, Grandma couldn't leave it at that. The pavlova rose again, this time it was huge, way above our heads.
Dad was trying to distract Mr. Janskee by asking him questions about the school, but it didn't work. He was

fascinated!

Mom took its size back down to normal height again and said, "Ah, just perfect. I've been experimenting with new castor sugar, so weird how it affected the pavlova." She quickly stuck a knife into it and started slicing...stopping Grandma from her little game.

By this stage, I think Dad's blood pressure must have been through the roof. He just sat there in silence. Everyone ate dessert and Mr. Janskee thanked my parents for a wonderful meal.

As "Kevvy" was about to leave, Grandma said, "It was a pleasure meeting you Kevin and she kissed him on the cheek."

He turned to her and asked, "Would you like to meet up for coffee tomorrow Thelma?"

This was way too much for Dad. He fainted. As his body hit the floor with a loud thump, everyone ran to his aid, except for Grandma and Kevvy, they stood there exchanging phone numbers and smiles.

Maybe I Went Too Far!

As soon as we arrived at school, Jordy ran up to Lindy.

"Hi beautiful, I came to school early, hoping to see you before class and it was fully worth getting up, you look amazing," he said, staring into her eyes.

Lindy smiled and asked, "How long have you been waiting, Jordy?"

Lowering his eyes, Jordy softly said, "Two hours...the gates were locked so I waited outside until the groundsman opened them up."

"Why would you do that?!" Lindy was obviously shocked.

A hurt look came over his face, "I was missing you."

Guilt was hitting me like a hammer. The poor guy, he was totally besotted to the point he was doing stupid things.

It was obvious that Lindy didn't know what to say or how to deal with a lovesick boy. "Are you okay Jordy?" she asked.

He looked into her eyes, revealing tears in his, "I am now Lindy."

He reached over and put his hand gently on her cheek. "You know you mean the world to me...you are my princess."

Normally Lindy would laugh at a comment like that, but the look on Jordy's face showed that he was totally sincere. "Come on Jordy, let's go to class," she said.

I sat first and Lindy quickly grabbed the seat next to me. Jordy sat behind up. English class was first up and our teacher asked us to take out last night's homework. We had to find a quote from someone who inspires us.

Miss Bart asked Lindy to read hers first. She chose John

Lennon.

"Being honest may not get you many friends, but it will always get you the right ones."

Wow, did she know more than she was letting on? The guilt factor just went up to extra high! I could feel my body heating up, my heart beating much faster, my hands felt wet and my face went RED!

I was next and I chose Nelson Mandela.

"It always seems impossible until it's done."

Lindy whispered, "Wow, that's deep sis."

I could feel breathing on the back of my neck, it was Jordy. "I love your quote Lindy, it is so you."

Copy Cat Cate was next. This must have been a hard task for her, as it was part of homework and she had to come up with her own ideas. But the quote she came up with had Lindy and I shocked and almost gagging.

"My famous person isn't some old dead person, it is Lady Gaga.
You have to be unique and different and shine in your own way."

Everyone in our class knows what Cate is like...nobody laughed, nobody clapped, they all sat there in stone cold silence until Miss Bart asked Jordy to stand and deliver his quote.

Jordy stood and looked at Lindy and said, "*If you find someone you love in your life, then hang onto that love.* It's a quote by Princess Diana and it really says how I feel." His eyes had not moved from Lindy's face. Once again, Jordy's quote was met with silence for at least 10 seconds.

Poison Ivy was the first to speak, "Are you serious Jordy? What's wrong with you?"

And then the whole class, except for Lindy, Jordy and myself, burst into laughter.

A horrified look came over Lindy's face. Her boyfriend moved closer to her and whispered, "Don't listen to them Lindy, they are just jealous."

As if in slow motion, it was that moment when Lindy realized that something was wrong and that I might be involved. She gave me a death stare and whispered, "You did something to him, didn't you?"

A slight nod of the head from me confirmed her suspicions. "Undo it!" she demanded.

Miss Bart was trying to regain everyone's attention. Jordy ignored her and leaned even closer to Lindy. "Your smell is intoxicating Lindy, how come you always smell so gorgeous?"

This time Lindy didn't whisper, she was serious, "NOW!"

I quickly reversed the spell. Jordy was only inches away from Lindy, his eyes flickered and then he stood up and rubbed his forehead before sitting down.

The lesson continued on, but I don't think I heard any more quotes, my mind was full of worry about the consequences of my little spell. Finally, the bell rang and everyone raced towards the door, except for my sister and me.

Tears running down her eyes, Lindy looked at me, "How could you do that to me? I feel like such a fool, I actually believed that he liked me!"

Trying to make it less painful for her, I said, "I'm sure he does like you Lindy, who wouldn't..." And that was where she cut me off.

"Don't you ever interfere with my life again! And if you do, I will never speak to you for the rest of your life. Do you understand me?" Lindy was now screaming. Lucky that Miss Bart is almost deaf!

With her embarrassment level at an all time high, Lindy refused to go to the lunch area, instead, we hung around the classroom and then visited the library until the next class.

Aww, So Cute!

My little social experiment didn't turn out to be a total failure after all!
When the going home bell rang and everyone ran for the door, Jordy held onto Lindy's arm and told her he needed to talk to her. I hung around, pretending I had dropped something on the floor.

Lindy thought she would beat him to the breaking-up part. "Jordy, I want to give you your friendship ring back. It's not you, it's me...I just feel that we were kind of thrown together, if you know what I mean."

I looked up to see his reaction. He put his hand out in a stop signal and said, "But why, I really like you Lindy and I thought you liked me too?"

A look of confusion showed on Lindy's face. She turned her face away from Jordy and looked down at me, raising her eyebrows. I shook my head to signal that I wasn't responsible for the comment.

And then something happened that melted Lindy's heart. It wasn't an over-the-top proclamation of love, but a simple solitary tear rolled down his cheek.

In a low, breaking voice, Jordy said, "I know that you are out of my league, I never imagined that a girl as beautiful and special as you would be interested in me..." He stopped talking, a lump in his throat.

Moving towards Jordy, Lindy reached out for his hand. "Actually Jordy, it is the opposite way round. I can't believe that someone as wonderful as you would like plain old me. That is why I was going to set you free. I thought you must have made a mistake."

I was mesmerized, this was the most gorgeous thing I had ever witnessed and it had nothing to do with a magic spell. This was real!

They hugged each other. It was like nobody else was in the room. Until...Miss Bart looked up and saw two of her 12-year-old students cuddling.

"What are you two doing?!" she demanded.

Jordy and Lindy immediately broke apart. "Arrr...nothing Miss Bart, Lindy was feeling sad about a personal situation and I was trying to be a good friend and make her feel better."

Miss Bart seemed to accept this and replied, "That's really nice of you Jordy, but try to comfort her in a less physical way." She smiled and waved them out of the classroom. I stood up from the floor and followed them out the door. As I passed Miss Bart, she winked at me. What did that mean?

Deputy Dad

Today was Dad's first day in his new job. We hadn't told any of our friends of the impending disaster to our social lives, secretly hoping that it would all go away or aliens would abduct us before it happened.

Walking to assembly we could see him standing on the stage, a huge bright smile beaming from his face. Mr. Janskee was next to him with his usual grumpy face, trying to work out the speaker system. Seriously, he has been Principal of this school forever and every week we go through the same thing with the sound system making strange noises, microphones screeching and turning on and off.

A loud bang rang through the hall.

Mr. Janskee had almost electrocuted himself. He jumped in the air, a look of horror on his face and I think I heard a naughty word escape from his mouth!

Lindy and I had purposefully got to assembly late and quickly sat down at the back of our class group...hoping nobody would see us. And Mr. Janskee's zap with the electricity helped to hide our sneaky entrance.

But that wasn't to last for long. Dad stepped in and plugged the microphone into the correct socket and then he stood up there, proud and tall, testing the microphone. There were gasps of surprise when our classmates saw our dad up there and then they all turned around to find us. We sank lower into our chairs, but Poison Ivy pointed us out to everyone.

"Well, if it isn't the twins' father up on stage. Girls, what is going on?" she asked, in a loud sarcastic tone.

What can you say to that?

Lindy eventually came up with some words, "It is only temporary, Dad is just helping out while Miss Jones is on holidays." And then she started to silently cry. I told you that my sister is a Drama Queen!

Jordy looked at Lindy and mouthed, "It's okay Lindy." But he was the only one who was sympathetic, everyone else either laughed or looked shocked.

We endured the assembly. About half way through the "Drama Queen" stopped crying when she realized that our father was a bit of a hit. Well, let's face it...Mr. Janskee was as boring as watching paint dry and our previous Deputy, Miss Jones, was mean and super sarcastic. Nobody liked her. And here was Dad, wowing the crowd with a story about when he was a young boy at school.

"When I was 10 years old, I had a teacher called Mrs. Johnson, she was old and cranky-looking like me. (This received a slight giggle from the students.) Up until this stage of my schooling, I was pretty hopeless at math. Okay not pretty hopeless, but totally failing. I found math impossible to understand and I had basically given up.

Then I was put into Mrs. Johnson's room. I told her to just leave me alone, I was a failure, dumb, hopeless. She walked away from me and continued on with the lesson about common fractions. When the bell rang everyone rushed outside, but she was waiting at the door and asked me to stay for a while. I thought, not another lecture about finishing my work on time. Mrs. Johnson told me that I didn't believe in myself, but she certainly did. And it was her mission to make me love math. I burst into laughter. Nobody, and I mean NOBODY, would ever make me like math.

She talked to me about what I liked to do on the weekends and I told her about my love of motorbikes. She asked me what I loved to eat and I told her that pizza was my favorite food, followed by sushi. Mrs. Johnson just listened to me. By the end of our discussion, I felt really comfortable talking to her. This was unusual, as teachers gave me the jitters and made me feel anxious.

The next day when I arrived at school, Mrs. Johnson had pizzas on the tables and cutting knives. We continued the lesson on fractions using the pizzas. And guess what everyone...this was the day that I finally understood fractions!

Mrs. Johnson turned my world around that day. She continued to teach in a way that inspired her students every day for the rest of the school year. And by the end of the year, I was confident, I loved school and I decided that when I grew up, I wanted to be a teacher so that I too could help kids.

Today, standing in front of you is the man who grew from that 10-year-old boy. I want you to know that I am here to help you. I want each and every one of you to flourish and feel confident. If you have a problem, my door is always open. And if you don't have a problem, then my door is still open for you, come and see me and let me get to know you as a person.

By sharing my story, I hope that all of you now know me a little better, and it is an absolute honor to be your Deputy Principal for the next term."

As soon as Dad stopped talking the whole school student body stood up and clapped loud and long. Kids in our class who were struggling with school, were crying and smiling at the same time. Even Mr. Janskee looked touched and he patted Dad on the back.

Dad had aced it! The kids who had been sniggering at us turned around with smiles and high fives.

"That's my Dad!" proclaimed Lindy the Drama Queen.

The Date

Today has been weird. And I mean weird with a capital W! Lindy and I have been trying to forget that our grandmother is going on a date with our school Principal. It still feels like we are having a bad (and I mean really bad) dream.

"I'm not sure about this hat," Grandma fussed in front of the mirror. She was changing hats with a snap of her fingers and so far, she had tried every style of hat available in the entire world!

Seriously Grandma...you are going out with Mr. Janskee, not Harry Styles!

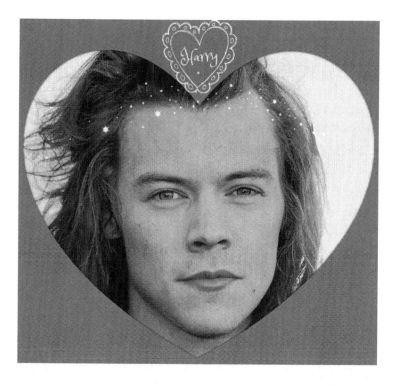

Grandma and Mom have totally different attitudes towards how to use their magic skills. Mom is really super-uptight about being a witch. And it is kind of refreshing to watch Grandma be so comfortable with her powers. "Poof," she laughed as the hat on her head changed color.

And after trying on all those hats, Grandma chose to go without a hat. "Girls, do you think my hair looks okay without a hat?" she asked. Lindy and I assured her that she looked great.

Then the next question came, "Does my bottom look big in this dress?"

"No bigger than normal," quipped Lindy. Grandma's head swung back towards the mirror.

I gave Lindy a *'say another word and I'll turn you into a frog'* look and tried to repair the damage. "She's only joking Grandma, your bottom looks fine."

"Fine, what does **fine** mean?" Now she was really losing it. After 5 hours of preparing for her date, Grandma was almost hysterical.

And that was when the doorbell rang. Mom walked into the room and came to the rescue, "Oh my goodness, you look beautiful, Kevin is one lucky man." Grandma's shoulders straightened a little and the frown disappeared from her forehead.

As Mom continued to reassure her mother, Lindy grabbed my arm and we ran to the front window to spy. This was going to be too good to miss. I mean, Grandma Thelma and Mr. Janskee!

"Kevvy!" We could hear Grandma gushing as she opened the door. Lindy and I looked at each other and tried to hold it together. We didn't want them to hear us laughing.

"What did I miss?" Mom asked as she sat down on the floor beside us. We were all crouching by the window staying as low as we could.

"She called him Kevvy and kissed him on the lips, not on the cheek, but right on the lips," Lindy whispered. Mom pretended to gag when we told her about the kiss.

"Before we leave Kevvy," Grandma said, and we all ducked down low again. "I just have to say goodbye to the girls. "Bye girls!" Busted! Grandma was looking right at us. "Stop hiding behind the curtain and say goodbye to Kevin and I," Grandma smiled, as we slowly stood up tall and waved awkwardly to them.

"What do think they're going to do?" Lindy asked as we watched the couple head towards Mr. Janskee's car.

"Have dinner?" It was more of a question than an answer, but I didn't really want to think about it.

"No, I mean," Lindy paused as she tried to come up with the right words. "I mean...he's not going to be our grandpa? It's embarrassing enough having our father at school!"

"I don't think we have to worry about that yet," Mom said, as she walked away. "This is only a first date. It could go really badly." That was a comforting thought. I wanted Grandma to be happy, and I guess Mr. Janskee being happy could be a good thing, but I wasn't sure I wanted them to be happy together. But I didn't feel as strongly as Lindy did about it.

"I hope it goes very badly," Lindy muttered. "I hope he farts and burps during dinner. I hope he tells her she has a big bottom. I hope his false teeth fall out into his soup. I hope his pants split and he has dirty underwear underneath."

"That's enough young lady!" Mom didn't sound very happy. "Your grandmother has been by herself for many years. If Kevin makes her happy, that is all we should care about. How can you be so selfish?"

Lindy lowered her head and sighed. But she didn't apologize, she turned and walked into our bedroom and closed the door. Poor Lindy, she didn't cope very well with changes, especially changes that put her social standing at extreme risk!

If this was a look into the future, it was scary. Mom and Dad sat on the couch, pretending to watch TV, but I could see that their eyes were focused on the driveway.

9:00 – Mom checked her phone.

9:30 – Dad checked his phone.

Lindy and I were sent to bed. "Grandma will be home soon," Mom said with conviction.

Of course, we weren't going to sleep until she got home, we wanted to hear all the juicy gossip! Lindy and I lay on the floor, commando style, listening to our parents and watching their movements through the space between the door and floor.

10:00 (Way past our parents' usual bedtime) Dad walked outside and looked down the street. What he was hoping to see, I have no idea!

11:30 Mom was quizzing Dad over what he knew about Kevvy.

I actually heard them use the terms "kidnapper" and "mad man." Then Mom wanted to call the hospitals (just in case they had been in an accident). Five minutes later she suggested calling the police. This was actually getting serious now.

My sister and I looked at each other. We share an ability to kind of read each other's minds and at that precise moment, we could see into the future. Our future! And dating was going to be difficult, extremely difficult, almost impossible! "Grandma is old, what are they going to be like with us?" said Lindy. I didn't have an answer, I just shrugged my shoulders and sighed.

Our parents were in full crisis mode. "Do people their age really need to be out this late?" Mom asked as she paced through the kitchen

"Why don't they call?" Dad said as he walked past the gap at the end of the hall and then disappeared again. "You should call your mother," he semi-demanded, as Mom walked into view again.

"I should call," Mom always repeated things when she didn't want to do them. "I should call, really? I believe it was your boss that came and picked up my mother?"

"Well, it's your mother..." Dad was searching for words. "She is your relative, and you can call her."

Mom was shaking her head angrily as she opened her phone. She held the phone to her ear but continued to shake her head. I wondered why she didn't just use a locate spell, but Mom didn't use magic unless she had to...especially in front of Dad. This was frustrating at times. "Straight to voicemail."

Dad sighed because he knew he had to call his boss now. Mom had tried, and it was now his turn. "Janskee's phone is off too." They sighed at each other and then the sound of car doors closing made them run for the window.

"Stay low," Mom cautioned Dad. "She's already caught me once today." Dad nodded to her and my parents crouched down to watch out of the front window. Lindy and I had a much narrower view under the bedroom door.

"They're kissing!" Mom almost yelled, but she caught herself.

"Ahhh!" We all softly screamed.

The door closed gently and Grandma walked in, stopped and looked straight at Mom and Dad.

"So I have a welcoming committee," Grandma Thelma laughed. "I had a great night, but you really didn't need to wait up."

"Where are you going?" Mom jumped up, she had that *'I'm not happy'* voice on. She had her hands on her hips, and she was giving grandma an evil-looking eye. "We've been waiting and worrying about you for the last four hours..."

"It felt like three minutes," Grandma smiled as she headed off to her room.

Mom wasn't finished yet. She followed Grandma to the guest bedroom.

I whispered to my sister, "Want to risk going out commando style, otherwise we won't be able to hear?" Lindy nodded and I quietly opened our door and we crawled down the hall.

"And why was your phone off?" Mom said sternly. It was the first thing that we heard as Lindy and I touched our ears to the wall.

"I guess that's what dating will be like," Lindy whispered. It was kind of funny, but it was also true. If Mom and Dad were this upset about Grandma dating, Lindy and I were in BIG trouble.

"What if we needed to get a hold of you?" Dad asked in his 'teachers' voice. We could actually hear Grandma's shock through the wall. Dad needed to get out of there now, questioning Grandma was not a good idea.

"Hazel can find me anytime she wants," Grandma sneered. She hated being reminded of her daughter's 'life choices' as Grandma always called them. She just couldn't understand why her daughter made such a big deal about magic. "Besides, what I do is none of your business."

The door slammed, and Mom and Dad were now suddenly in the hall. "Did she just float us out of our own guest room?" Dad asked. Mom started to yell, but Grandma shut it right down and only little mouse like squeaks came from her mouth.

"Oh and thanks for asking if I had a nice time." Grandma's sarcasm was dripping right through the walls.

Mom huffed and then my parents stomped off in the other direction down the hall. They were so angry, they didn't even notice us lying in the hall. We could hear them arguing in whispered tones in the kitchen again, but we couldn't make out the words.

Grandma opened her door and said, "Go to bed now girls, the show is over."

Lindy and I quickly crawled back to our bedroom and hopped into our beds. It had been a very eventful night.

"Would you use magic on a date?" Lindy asked. I was staring up at the glowing plastic stars on our ceiling. I wanted to say no, but I really wasn't sure, was using magic really as wrong as Mom made it seem?

Soon afterward we both fell asleep. Spying under the door was tiring work.

***

The next morning we found out that her date went well. Mom still looked a little tense, but Dad was smiling. Mr. Janskee took Grandma to a fancy café by the lake. Apparently, everything was perfect, except for a strong breeze that was going to mess up Grandma's hair. She told us how she snapped her fingers and it calmed down.

Mom groaned for weeks about that one. People everywhere (in the shops, at work, in the park) kept talking about the strange weather. Mr. Oanafsky, the butcher, told us, "Can you believe it, one minute it was windy, and the next nothing!" Mom tried to be polite, but I could tell she was boiling underneath it all. She took the use of magic very seriously.

Grandma continued on with her story. After they sat down, Kevvy ordered a milkshake, Grandma loved that he had a milkshake, "It was so, hip," she gushed. Lindy and I looked at each other and mouthed the word, 'hip' in disbelief. Our Principal, hip? Grandma Thelma even wiped the ice cream off of Mr. Janskee's mustache, ick! It seemed to make her happy, but it made me gag.

The only problem they had, was that at the restaurant there was a disgusting smell. At first, Grandma thought it was Kevy, and he thought it was her. They both tried to excuse the other person, and politely suggest a trip to the bathroom to freshen up. But neither of them seemed to get the hint.

"It smells like someone has stepped in dog poo," Kevvy finally said, sniffing at the air.

He took the lead and got up. As he walked away from the table, Grandma Thelma saw some dog poo stuck to the underside of Kevy's shoe.

She laughed to herself and poofed the problem away.

She used her magic at the movie theatre. Kevvy noticed something strange, he said to Grandma, "Everyone who tries to sit in front of us seems to stop and then turn and walk away, it's like magic or something." He laughed and said, "It must be our lucky day!"

Grandma Thelma laughed it off.

She laughed until the movie started. Grandma Thelma had a hard time with the movie they chose. It was about the Salem Witch Trials, and it got to Grandma, for obvious reasons. "He put his arm around me," Grandma told me later. (In my head I was begging her not to.)

Excitement in the Air!

When the twins walked into assembly they could sense a buzz in the air. A rumor was racing around the room, like a blowfly circling a rotten piece of meat. And the rumor was that the school was going to hold a dance soon!!!

Lindy and I looked at each other. We were very doubtful. Dad hadn't mentioned anything about an upcoming dance and being the children of one of the teachers at the school, we had heard conversations about what happened at the last dance and how the school staff never wanted another one to be held.

Mom and Grandma had been helping in the canteen, serving food and drinks and they actually saw the mayhem. Mom said the number of teacher injuries was enormous. The twist put three hips out...the limbo wrecked four backs and there were even three black eyes and a broken nose from the Macarena!

Most of the staff were away the following week. Mr. Janskee had to employ teachers from miles around to replace his fallen staff.

As they returned, the teachers didn't know what had come over them to make them act in such foolhardy ways. Mrs. Spoodle said that she hadn't danced for over 40 years and had no idea why she wanted to win the Twist Dance competition...she was away for a lot longer with her hip replacement surgery.

Jordy's head was swinging from the right to the left, looking around the hall. As soon as he spotted Lindy, he jumped up and quickly ran towards her with a huge smile on his face. "Great news Lindy, there's going to be a dance and I want you to be my partner!"

Immediately Lindy forgot about her reservations on whether the school would actually have another dance. "Jordy! I'd love to be your partner at the dance, it's going to be fantastic!"

I nudged her in the ribs. But Lindy was in the *staring into the eyes of the cutest boy in the universe'* mode and she wasn't going to be distracted.

The microphone screeched. Yes, it was Kevvy again, surely after all these years he knew how to turn it on without causing everyone to cringe. But...maybe he did it on purpose to get our attention?

"Sit down everyone and be quiet," he bellowed. Same words as always. He started the assembly with all the usual boring stuff and as the parade was about to end and every student was waiting in anticipation, he finally had a quiet chuckle to himself before saying, "A few years ago we had a dance that went terribly wrong. Everyone groaned. "And as you all know, we haven't had one since then." Silence. "Our new Deputy Principal has convinced me that we should try another school dance."

The whole school, except for the teachers, jumped into the air, cheering and celebrating.

Yes, our Dad was a hit again!

He screeched the microphone again, confirming my suspicions. "Of course, that decision could be changed." Everyone immediately sat down quietly.

"The dance will be held on Friday week in the assembly hall. The theme shall be fancy dress, you can wear anything you want, as long as it is appropriate." Whispering broke out. He screeched the microphone again.

"But let me warn you...any misbehavior and you will not be allowed to attend and if you play up on the night, your parents will be called to pick you up." Mr. Janskee was sounding very serious.

As soon as he dismissed assembly, the gossip started. Who would ask a date to the dance? What would everyone wear...and who would be banned from the dance?

Straight after school on the day of the big announcement, Poison Ivy asked Lindy's boyfriend to be her date! And she did it in front of Lindy!
Jordy was horrified! He looked at her, then he looked at Lindy, and finally, after turning a vivid shade of red, he replied, "No, Ivy, I don't want to be your date. Didn't you know that Lindy is my girlfriend?"

Jordy sounded shocked and astounded, while Lindy just stood there with a steely look of hate on her face and her arms tightly folded.

Seriously, one day Ivy will win an acting award, maybe even an Oscar. She looked at Jordy and pretended she was shocked. "Are you kidding me!" she said. "To be honest, I had heard a rumor, but I told my friend that she was delusional, I told her that Jordy would never go out with Lindy, she is way too uncool for him. But it looks like my friend was right."

Then she looked at Jordy and Lindy and said, "Sorry you two, I really had no idea."

"As if..." Lindy huffed, before walking off. Jordy frowned and shook his head, without saying another word to Ivy, he took off after Lindy.

As soon as Jordy had turned away, Poison Ivy smiled. It was obvious that she had known all along.

I sent a little spell her way. An upset stomach doesn't help with someone who is trying to be cool. Ivy's stomach started to grumble, it started with a gurgling noise that gradually got louder and louder...and then Ivy let off a humongous ripper of a fart. Seriously this fart went for about 5 seconds, it kept going on and on and on. Everyone around her stopped and looked at her. She pretended that she had rubbed the side of her shoe on the ground. Then came the second one, even louder and longer, and surprise, her foot wasn't moving at all. Giggles erupted and her face reddened as she quickly walked off towards the toilets holding her stomach.

The next day, Ivy was absent, apparently, she had some type

of food poisoning. I reversed the spell, hoping that she had learned a lesson.

***

Over the next two weeks, dates were made and broken and remade. But Jordy and Lindy remained strong and even coordinated their outfits. Jordy suggested that they go as a witch and wizard so that their costumes would have a common theme. At first, Lindy was a bit hesitant as she knew that our father wouldn't like it. But the look of excitement on Jordy's face was enough to make her forget about her somewhat strange family makeup and she agreed.

Lindy smiled and winked at me, "Great idea Jordy. But don't witches look ugly with green skin, big ugly noses, and warts?"

Fighting off the urge to tackle my sister to the ground, I replied, "Well you won't have to wear too much makeup then, will you Lindy!" And I poked my tongue at her.

Jordy looked from one twin to the other with a quizzical look on his face.
Quickly changing the subject, Lindy asked me what I was going to wear. I smiled, "It's a surprise, you'll have to wait until the dance night to find out."

Copy Cat Cate skipped over and joined in the conversation. "What are you two girls dressing up as?"

Before I could stop her, Lindy replied, "I'm going as a witch."

As usual, not showing an ounce of originality, Copy Cat Cate replied, "That's a great idea! I've been struggling to think of something to wear and my older sister has a great witch costume at home. I'll go as a witch too! It will be so much fun, we'll be like twins!"

The real twins groaned.

***

Do you know how long two weeks can take!!!! And how many dramas can erupt in that time!!!! Cindy certainly had her work cut out. Mr. Janskee had warned that the dance would be canceled if there was any bad behavior in the school.

So when graffiti appeared on the toilet wall...Cindy was there, instantly removing it.

The rubbish on the ground miraculously disappeared at the end of every eating session throughout the fortnight.
Kids who were thinking about skipping school and walking away from the front gate...suddenly turned around and headed into their classroom.

A couple of boys who were famous for swearing, could not bring themselves to say a swear word...nothing came out.

Yes, Cindy was REALLY BUSY!

On the Friday of the school dance, Cindy sat in her normal seat for our science lesson. She looked up, just in time to see that Craig and Col (the two naughtiest boys in our class) had set up a bucket of water to fall on Mr. Gordon's head as he walked into the classroom. She lifted her hand to command the bucket not to fall...but, she was too late and half the water had already landed on Mr. Gordon's clothing.

Everyone gasped! They knew what the consequence of this foolish action would be!

And then in reverse, each drop drained from his clothing and flew back into the bucket. And then Mr. Gordon walked backward out of the classroom. I looked at my sister and winked.

Then everyone in the room froze. The twins quickly hopped out of their seats, pulled over a chair and lifted the bucket off the door and poured the water down the sink. They returned to their seats.

"How did you do that?" Lindy asked.

Cindy giggled, "A simple backward time spell, actually I didn't know if it would work, my first time using it. Shall we unfreeze them?"

Lindy smiled, "Maybe, although it is nice and quiet in here for a change."

With a wave of her arm, the whole class woke up. Some kids yawned, while others rubbed their foreheads. Craig and Col looked up at the top of the door. The bucket was no longer balanced on the top of the doorway. The boys looked very puzzled.

Then Mr. Gordon walked in as if nothing had happened. Disaster averted!

The Dance

Did I tell you that Grandma Thelma and Kevvy are still dating?
I personally try not to think about it!

Dad came home late from work, he had been helping to set up the decorations in the hall for tonight's dance. He already looked exhausted. Mom was at home packing plastic cups, serviettes and tongs to take to the dance canteen. Tonight was going to be so cool. Pizza, soda, music, and dancing...what more could a kid ask for?

The door bell rang and I raced to answer it, hoping it would be one of my friends showing off their outfit...but no, it was Grandma Thelma.

She kissed me on the cheek, which meant that I now had red lips on my face. "How's my beautiful little witch girl?" Grandma asked in a rather loud voice. She obviously didn't realize that my father was home...or did she?

"I'm great Grandma, can't wait for tonight, it is going to be so exciting," I said in a loud voice. Then quietly I added, "Mom and Dad are in the kitchen." She gave me a wink.

"Hazel, Bruce, never fear, Grandma Thelma is here! So, how can I help?" she called out.

Help? Was Grandma coming to the dance?

Thump, thump, thump...I heard Dad storming out of the kitchen. "Oh no, you're NOT!" Dad was actually yelling. "Not after the last time!"

"Oh don't be so stuffy Bruce! I've learned my lesson and

besides, you have to admit that your boring staff has never had so much fun."

Dad was fuming. He opened his mouth to start yelling at Grandma, but nothing came out.

"You will listen to me Brucey Boy. Kevvy has asked me to help and I will not let him down. And I won't let you down. No weirdo magic, I promise," she said, before waving her hand.

Dad didn't say a word. He knew he had lost this argument and he stormed off to his bedroom to get ready for the night.

After he had left, Mom peeked her head around the corner and softly said, "Make sure you keep that promise, we don't want a repeat of the last dance!"

Grandma smiled.
Lindy and I looked at each other. Was Grandma involved in the chaos at the last school dance?

***

It was now time to get dressed. Lindy had hired a witch costume for the night and she looked amazing. Jordy would be super impressed.

I put my princess outfit on and looked in the mirror. Wow, I really looked like a princess from a fairy tale. I looked so grown up!

Mom allowed us to wear makeup to the dance. Both of us have naturally long and dark eyelashes, but putting eyeliner around our eyes was so hard! Lindy made a real mess of her face. Her eyes looked totally different. She looked in the mirror and burst into tears, making it look even worse!

"Cindy, use your magic!" she demanded. "Please!"

I took another look at her eyes and agreed. Within seconds her face looked like a professional makeup artist had applied the perfect eyeliner, pink eyeshadow, and red lipstick.

Then I did my own...with a little help, of course! Perfect!

We gave each other a hug and walked out to show our costumes to our waiting family. Dad burst into tears, he is such a softie! Mom and Grandma smiled and told us that we looked amazing. Then we all headed off to the dance.

***

Jordy was waiting for Lindy at the door. Such a gentleman! "Oh Lindy, you look fantastic!" he gushed.

He was super impressed. And right in front of Dad and Mom, he took Lindy's hand and led her onto the dance floor. It was so romantic!

Meanwhile, I just hung around hoping that someone would ask me to dance....anyone! Yes, there I was, Cindy the Loser, checking out her nails over and over again. I even started to count how many boys were standing around and NOT dancing. After a while, I was tempted to just give up and go and help Mom and Grandma in the canteen. But then I looked up and before me stood Harry. Tall, strong and handsome...Harry was our year level number one jock. Lindy and I called him Hunky Harry. And he was standing in front of me, looking at me and then his mouth opened.

"Hi Cindy, would you like to dance?" he said in a confident voice.

I was so shocked that when I opened my mouth to say yes, a flurry of words spewed out. "Thank God you asked me, I've been standing here all alone for ever and I thought nobody would ask me to dance and I was starting to feel really upset..."

Harry put his finger gently across my mouth. "It's okay Cindy, let's get onto the dance floor and show them how it's done."

I was the princess and he had saved me. And he was even dressed as a super hero! Hunky Harry had rescued me from the embarrassment of not dancing at the school dance. And for that...I adored him!

At this moment in time, everything in my world was fantastic. This was my first school dance...and I was certain, it would be my best school dance ever. Harry and I had been dancing for at least an hour. He was so perfect, funny and great to be with.

The limbo sticks came out and Harry and I were doing really well. Both of us had made it to the final 10 contestants. As I bent backward to conquer another level...in the corner of my eye, I saw a pizza flying through the air. It was swooping high above the kids and then it made a sharp turn towards the canteen. I stood up immediately, there had to be magic involved in that flying pizza.

"Oh no, Cindy is out!" came the announcement.

Harry came over and gave me a hug, "Sorry princess, looks like I'll have to win for both of us." And he raced back into line, ready to take his turn.

So sweet!!!!! How come I had never really taken any notice of Harry before tonight? Maybe because he was one of the popular kids and I was, well, just me. Then another pizza flew through the air and I watched it head back to the canteen. Time to investigate!

Looking around, Mom was nowhere to be seen. Grandma was manning, or should I say witching, the serving area. She was throwing pizzas to entertain the kids who were lined up waiting for their slice.

"So who's for pepperoni?" she asked, as a pizza landed in front of her.

A dozen kids all called out and put their hands in the air. Copy Cat Cate grabbed me and yelled excitedly in my ear, "Your Grandma is the coolest granny in the world!"

Yes, I did have to admit; she was putting on quite a show

and entertaining everyone. Pizzas were whizzing in and out of the oven and some were flying around the hall. But that was when Dad walked over, he had obviously seen the pizzas flying around the room as well.

"Thelma!" he said firmly. "Can I speak to you for a moment?" I was pretty proud of Dad, he was keeping it together...just!

Raising her eyebrows, Grandma replied, "Of course, Brucey." All the kids in the line burst into laughter.

He took her arm and led her out to the back. I could hear raised voices, but the words were muffled and difficult to hear because of the loud music in the background. The kids waiting in the pizza line were all quiet now, trying to hear what they were saying.
And then my mother reappeared. She looked around searching for Grandma and a look of panic spread over her face. I looked at her and made a face, nodding my head and mouthed the words, "Flying pizzas" and "Dad's with her now". My eyes indicated that they were out the back.

Mom immediately put a holding spell over the whole hall, every person froze, except for those of us who are witches. We quickly walked to the back of the canteen and found Dad, anger frozen all over his face and his finger pointing at Grandma.

"You're doing it again!" Mom yelled.

A huge sigh escaped from Grandma's mouth, "Oh darling, it was getting so boring, I just thought I'd add some excitement to serving up pizzas. And besides, the kids loved it!"

Mom didn't say a word, but she turned her back to her mother and then she started to sob. Grandma had gone too far...again.

"I'm sorry honey," Grandma tried to console my mom.

And this was when Mom exploded, "I trusted you! You promised me! Don't you realize you could ruin Bruce's career!"
Slinking back, Grandma told Mom that she would fix everything and she put a lose-your-memory for the last half hour spell on every normal in the building. So not only did Dad have no memory of their argument, but the kids couldn't remember seeing flying pizzas either. "There you go, all fixed," she said, with a smile on her face.

Mom still wasn't happy, "I want you to go home, step out of the canteen and don't come back in here."

Grandma knew she was in all sorts of trouble with my mother. She nodded agreement and walked outside, then Mom waved her arms unfreezing everyone. At first, there was stark silence, only the music could be heard. Everyone seems to shake their heads and rub their eyes, before resuming what they were doing beforehand.

Dad looked at Mom, "Hi my gorgeous wife, how's it going?" Phew, he was in a good mood again.

Mom smiled and told him that everything was running smoothly, but that her mother was tired and she was going home. Grandma didn't say a word, she just waved at Dad and walked out of the canteen.

As she was walking towards the exit door, Mr. Janskee spotted her leaving. He actually ran after her and caught her at the door. "Thelma, where are you going?" he asked.

"Kevvy, I'm a little tired. Lifting all those pizzas is hard work for an old girl like me." Seriously there was something regal about Grandma. Lindy and I often joked about how she should have been a queen...okay, maybe a drama queen!

He held out his hand and wrapped it around her back and gave her a cuddle. Mr. Janskee was cuddling my grandmother in front of the whole school population! Okay, perhaps only a few kids had witnessed it, but I knew that this gossip would spread like wildfire! How embarrassing, they were acting like lovesick teenagers!

Kevvy took her by the hand onto the dance floor and they started to dance to a Bieber song! Grandma actually looked pretty groovy, but Kevvy...he was attracting more and more attention, he moved like a baby hippo. But then all of a sudden the music changed! And it wasn't a good change!

Whitney Houston's voice blasted across the hall. "I will always love you..." Hmmmm...why was the DJ playing such an old-fashioned, love-sick song?

All the kids stopped dancing and looked at each other, bursting into laughter. Grandma and Kevvy didn't! Everyone formed a circle around them as they waltzed around the dance floor. He twirled her around and stared into her eyes.

"Isn't that your grandmother?" asked Poison Ivy, in a very loud voice.
Everyone near us turned towards Lindy and I and gasped, then they burst into laughter. Grandma was killing my cool factor!

Then Harry walked over and announced, "I wish my grandmother was that cool!" It is amazing how a comment from one of the 'in' kids can turn a situation around. Heads started nodding and faces began smiling.

At the end of the song, Kevvy held Grandma as he took her into a low back bend. The crowd erupted into applause. The two oldies smiled and Kevvy bowed while Grandma blew everyone a kiss.
The DJ put on another song, thankfully this one was a lot more modern and fast paced. Jordy dragged Lindy onto the floor and Harry and I closely followed them. We all danced in a little circle for the next hour. Hot and sweaty, we all went over to grab a soda.

Poison Ivy walked over as well. She had dressed as a devil. She did look good, but she didn't look as gorgeous as my sister Lindy. As Lindy turned to pour some soda into a cup, Ivy swooped in and stood very close to Jordy.

"Oh Jordy, you are such a great dancer...in fact, I think you are the best dancer in the school," said Ivy, fluttering her eyelashes.

Lindy tried to move closer to Jordy, but Ivy stood between them and squeezed her out. She continued on, "I've hardly had a dance tonight. Lindy, you wouldn't mind if I drag Jordy onto the dance floor for just one dance, would you?"

Jordy looked stunned, he obviously didn't know what to say. Lindy also looked shocked, but she managed to say, "Sure Ivy, but only if Jordy wants to dance with you." I personally think this was mean of my sister, putting it all back onto Jordy.

Jordy's mouth opened and stayed opened, no words came out.

"So I'm guessing that is a yes Jordy, come on!" Ivy dragged

Jordy onto the dance floor. As he was being pulled along, he looked back at Lindy and mouthed, "Save me!"

Tears came to Lindy's eyes. She looked at me, her mouth pouting and her forehead creased. A soft voice squeaked from her straight lips, "Help me, Cindy, please."

I looked over at Ivy, she was outrageously flirting with poor Jordy and touching him constantly. Anger rose in my throat and I focused on her forehead. Horns started growing...at first they were tiny bumps, but eventually, they looked like horns that you would see in a fairy tale book.

Jordy stopped dancing and stared at her. Of course, at first she thought he was just checking her out because of her beauty. But after a couple of minutes, she spotted what he was staring at.

The horns had become so large, that she could see them with her own eyes. She clamped her hands over them and ran into the bathroom.

"Thanks, Cindy," whispered Lindy.

When Jordy returned he couldn't stop talking about how these weird bumps had formed on her head, in front of his eyes. "They looked like real horns!"

Cindy walked into the bathroom to check on her. Ivy had locked herself in a cubicle and was crying.

"Are you okay Ivy?" Cindy asked.

At first, there was no response. Then after a large sniffle, Ivy replied, "NO I'm not! Something has happened to my forehead, it must be an allergic reaction. It is probably from those stupid pizzas your pathetic family served up."

Cindy smiled. At first, she had felt a little guilty, but after that comment...all sympathy had vanished. "Do you want me to go and tell a teacher?" Cindy asked.

"DON'T TELL ANYONE!" was her response. "I've called my mother and she is coming to pick me up and take me home, so leave me alone!"

Cindy decided to do just that and she walked out.

***

By Monday morning Ivy's horns had reduced to small bumps on her head, it looked like she had knocked her head badly. It was obvious that she had makeup on to try to cover them up, but nothing would cover the size. She looked like she had two small eggs on her head.

Lindy overheard Ivy talking to her friends. "The doctors have no idea what caused the lumps. But Mom and I think it was those disgusting pizzas the twins' mother served up at the dance."

Lindy walked over to me and gave me a fist pump. "She asked for it, well-done Sis!"

Dance Awards

During lunch on Monday, everyone was full of gossip about Friday night's dance. The students were still buzzing from the excitement and they all (except for Ivy) thought the night was a huge success.

And the best news of all was that Harry, yes –Hunky Harry – was paying heaps of attention to me at school. Yes ME! He even sat next to me during lunch. And Harry and Jordy seem to get along really well. Aaahh...sometimes life is perfect!

The senior students in the Student Council always give out awards after a dance on a special parade held on the first school day after the dance. Lindy and I were quietly hoping Poison Ivy would get an award for having the best horns. Everyone was making their predictions for the best couple, best dancers, and best-dressed awards.

Poor Miss Burt had no chance of any of us remembering the history lesson she gave to us prior to assembly. We were all too excited.

Finally, the announcement came over the PA system: All classes please proceed to the assembly hall for our special Dance Awards.

Normally our class hates going to assembly! They skulk around and walk as slowly as possible, but not today.

The female School Captain started the announcements. She thanked the school admin for allowing us to have a dance again and commented on how well behaved everyone was.

This brought about a huge cheer.

"Okay, the moment we have all been waiting for...the Best Dressed Award goes to Harry Grasso for his Super Hero outfit. Well done Harry, can you come up on stage?"

I felt so proud, Harry, *my* Harry had won the Best Dressed. He did look amazing and very handsome in his outfit. Harry walked up onto the stage and flexed his muscles, everyone cheered loudly.

Billy, the male school captain was next. "And the Best Dancing Award goes to...Bryce and Savannah." They were older kids and I do have to admit, they were pretty good. Although I was really hoping that Harry and I might have had a chance.

Then the two school Captains stood together to announce the final award. "And the Best Couple goes to...Mr. Janskee and Ms. Loyd." Cheers erupted and a Mexican wave of hats flew into the air.

Ms. Loyd...Oh my gosh, they were talking about Grandma! I looked at Mr. Janskee's face, he was blushing, but smiling at the same time.

The Captains continued, "We'd like to give you this award Mr. Janskee because you taught everyone that it doesn't matter how old you are, you can still be in love and have a good time."

LOVE!!!! Did they say, LOVE??? Lindy and I were in total shock! So was Dad! He looked like he had just woken from a terrible nightmare or like he had just sucked on a lemon, his face was all screwed up. We couldn't cheer, we just stood there watching it all unfold.

Mr. Janskee walked over to the Captains and accepted the award and then he took hold of the microphone.

"Please just finish the parade, please just finish the parade, please just finish the parade..." mumbled Lindy over and over again. I think she had gone into shock.

The microphone screeched. "Thank you, everyone for this award and yes (he looked at the Captains) you are right, nobody is ever too old to find love and have a great time."

Then it was my turn to mumble: "Please Earth, open up and swallow me."

But he wasn't finished! Oh no, he had more to say.

"I am so fortunate to have met my soul mate, a beautiful woman and a wonderful grandmother to the twins, Lindy and Cindy Thompson. You never know, one day I might even be their Step-Grandfather."

This absolutely sent every student into hysterics...everyone found this to be hilarious, except for us. We were mortified!

And then the bell rang. Time for dismissal and time for escape! Lindy and I rushed out of the hall. Everyone else was hanging around and talking about the awards. Not us, we were out in seconds.

"Cindy, use your magic and get us home now!" demanded Lindy. For once, Lindy and I were in total agreement. We disappeared and left Dad at school. I did feel a little guilty leaving him behind, but that's life. Sometimes you just have to save yourself!

The Invitation

"I got an invitation! I got an invitation!" Lindy was jumping for joy, holding firmly onto a piece of paper. Her joy and smile were contagious!

Eventually, after 5 seconds or so, I couldn't stand it any longer and put a still spell on her. "An invitation to where?" I asked.

"You'll never guess!!!" Lindy squealed. "Go on, guess!!!"

"Is it to a birthday party?" I asked.

"Correct!"

"Is it to a party for someone you like?" was my second question.

"YES!" came her excited reply.

I took the spell off her and she continued to jump up and down.

"It is going to be so much fun!" she yelled. "You're invited too!" Lindy showed me the invitation that had both our names on it.

Jordy's 13th BD Party

Lindy and Cindy

You're invited to Jordy's Birthday Party!
Date: 23 August
Time: 1pm to 4pm
Venue: Ice Skating Rink
Dress Warmly

RSVP to Jordy

"Yay!!!!" I was super excited. Not as excited as Lindy, but close.

When she settled down, Lindy said to me, "There's only one problem Cindy...we don't know how to ice skate." Boy, was that an excitement crusher!

I smiled, "I've got a solution..."

Lindy immediately cut me off. "No witch stuff Cindy! I know I asked for your help at the dance, but if you keep doing witch stuff, people will start to notice there is something strange about our family. Promise me!"

What a kill joy, she was more like Dad than I had realized. "Okay Lindy, no spells or magic, I promise."

***

The next day at school everyone in our class was buzzing with news about the upcoming Birthday Party. Jordy had a huge smile on his face as everyone RSVP'd saying that they would love to come.

And then Poison Ivy walked up to him. She put her hand out and swept his fringe off his forehead. "Hey Jordy, I'd love to come to your party, thanks for the invite." Then she turned and looked straight at Lindy and smirked.

Jordy didn't notice this, he was busy talking to Will about the party.

Holding her head close to mine, Lindy whispered, "Why did he have to invite her?"

I shrugged my shoulders. How was I supposed to know how Jordy's mind worked. But it soon became obvious that Jordy had invited everyone in the class. Typical of him, he is so kind, he wouldn't want to make anyone feel left out.

Unfortunately, my sister wasn't interested in seeing how considerate Jordy was, and she sulked for the rest of the day. At lunch time, Jordy asked, "Are you okay Lindy?" He looked genuinely concerned.

Lifting her head, she looked at him and gave a half-hearted smile. "Sure Jordy, I'm fine." Yes, the stock standard response from a girl who is NOT fine at all. Older men around the world know to be wary when a female says she is fine, but Jordy was only 12, soon to be 13, and he had no idea what "fine" actually meant.

"Cool," he replied. "Lindy, we are going to have so much fun at the skating rink. My parents are super keen to meet you, I've told them all about you."

Lindy's smile instantly changed from 'fake' to 'wow, you told your parents about me – happy smile'. "I can't wait to meet them too, Jordy. If they are as nice as you, I know I'll love them."

Oh my goodness, she just said the L word! Okay, it was about his parents, but even so...

Lindy and Jordan's little world was back on track. Totally forgetting about Poison Ivy, Lindy was happy again.

The Birthday Party

We arrived dressed in our warm clothes, excited about the adventure ahead. Lindy chose her outfit straight away, she has this gray pullover that she absolutely loves. It took me forever, okay at least 10 minutes. Lindy assured me that I didn't look like I belonged under the Christmas tree...eventually.

Together we bought Jordy a new PlayStation game, something about wars...why do boys love those games? Anyway, as predicted, he loved it!

Then it was time for everyone to be given ice skates, so we formed a line and patiently waited. Of course, who would have their own skates?

YES! You guessed it! Poison Ivy! And she looked amazing in a cute little skating outfit. She glided past us, "See you on the rink girls!" she called out, pretending she was being friendly. We knew better!

"It looks fairly easy," commented Lindy. Yes, my sister was delusional at that stage.

I just nodded. I could feel fear rising up my spine. Listening to the conversations around us, it appeared that everyone else had skated before. That is, except us!

The skating attendant pulled out some huge big white skates and plonked them onto Lindy's feet. "Make sure you tie them up tightly," he warned. They looked nothing like the petite light blue skates that Ivy wore.

Next, he brought out my skates. They made Lindy's ones look like they came from a high-end fashion store. My skates were gray with scuff marks all over them. I think that they were originally white, twenty years ago!

"Hey, skater boy, can I have a better pair please?" I asked with a smile on my face.

He didn't even look at me, "Sorry, the last pair, it's them or nothing."

Great!

Then I saw Hunky Harry walk in late.

He was carrying his own skates and although they weren't blue or petite, they certainly looked professional. He saw me and came over. "Hi, Cindy! Get those skates on and I'll take you for a whiz around the rink. See you out there."

I watched him enter the rink. He started skating, then spun around so he was skating backward! He blew me a kiss and waved for me to hurry up.

This was a true dilemma. Yes, I had promised Lindy that

there would be no witchcraft at the party. BUT...I was going to look like the world's biggest freak with my arms and legs totally out of control!

Lindy and I finished lacing our skates at the same time. We looked into each other's eyes. "No!" she said.

Drat! She had read my mind before I could even put forward an argument.

Holding onto the rail I stood up. My legs felt wobbly beneath me and my arms tensed to keep my body upright. My stubborn sister was just as unstable. We made it onto the rink, but I didn't dare let go. Poison Ivy glided past me and laughed. Aaargh!

Then Hunky Harry pulled up alongside me. "So Cindy, I'm guessing this is your first time on skates?" I smiled at him. What could I say?

"Hold my hand and I'll take you around the rink," he said with a confident smile. But as soon as I let go of the railing, my legs slipped from under me and I fell to the floor. Both my legs were in the air in a most unladylike position.

I looked over and Lindy was also on the ground, holding her head. Jordy was trying to pick her up, but Lindy was so uncoordinated that she slid into his legs and knocked him over as well.

Lindy looked over at me and mouthed, "DO IT!"

It can get a little frustrating being told what to do by your twin sister all the time. Especially when she gives you lectures and forbids you to use your special skills.

I mouthed back, "DO WHAT?" Pretending that I had no idea what she was talking about.

Harry was starting to pull me to my feet. I had to act quickly, but it was hard to think of a spell when you are under that much pressure! Not wanting to make it obvious that we have changed from being absolutely dreadful to super stars of the ice...I put a stability spell on both of us. This worked perfectly and both Lindy and I were able to stand and slowly skate around the rink. So much for – *NO Magic Lindy*!

This was definitely the best party ever! Jordy and Lindy...Harry and me, what more could a set of twins ask for?

Then the attendant interrupted the music, "Okay folks, it's time for some games! First up, only backward skaters can stay on the rink, everyone else can sit this song out."

There was no way that I could skate backward, going forwards was hard enough, so Lindy and I sat down and watched. It was a silly game. Everyone had to skate backward and when the music started and the girls had to catch a boy. After a minute, any girls who hadn't caught a boy were instantly out. Of course, you know what happened! Yes, Ivy went straight for Jordy, she caught him within 10 seconds! I could see Lindy's knuckles bracing onto the rail and turning white.

Lindy looked at me and said, "Why does she always have to flirt with my boyfriend?" I raised my eyebrows and nodded my head. What could I say?

Harry was still free and racing around the rink, avoiding the girls trying to capture him.

The music started again and several girls had to exit the rink as they hadn't been able to catch a boy. In fact, only four girls were still in the game. Jordy took off and so did Harry. It was obvious that Poison Ivy wanted to catch Jordy again. She had several opportunities to catch other boys, including Harry, but she let them go and focused on Lindy's boyfriend.

And then she caught him. Lindy sighed. Ivy was the only girl to catch a boy in that round, so she was the winner. She and Jordy were called to the center of the rink and told to get down on one knee. The attendant, whom I didn't like in the first place, placed a prince crown on Jordy's head and a princess crown on Ivy.

Before this happened, Lindy's knuckles were white, now the railing was starting to shake. She looked at me and whispered, "Ramp up our skills sis!"

I smiled. "Okay, I'll try to not make our miraculous improvement too obvious!" A spell swirled around our bodies. I stood on one foot, jumped into the air, did the splits...yes, the spell worked.

Jordy skated over to Lindy, with Poison Ivy following close behind.

An announcement came over the loud speaker that normal skating would resume.

Grabbing Lindy's hand, Jordy carefully helped her to get back onto her feet and led her onto the rink. As soon as they started to skate, Lindy spun around backward. The look on Jordy's face was one of shock! "Wow Lindy, you are such a fast improver. You must have natural balance and skills, it took me a year before I could do that."

Lindy spun around again and just in time. Nasty Ivy was standing with one foot out, waiting to trip Lindy. But Lindy's reactions were so quick now that she simply jumped over her extended leg. Lindy turned and gave her a smug look.

Another announcement: Could Jordy's friends please go the table area, a birthday cake and some yummy food are waiting for you. And then he sang Happy Birthday to Jordy. The cake had so many candles on it...13! Jordy made a silent wish and bent down to blow out his candles.

But before he had a chance, someone else blew four of them out. Jordy stopped and laughed, "Okay who blew out my candles?" Everyone laughed and nobody owned up.

He took in another breath. Before he could let it out, three more candles blew out. The first time it happened there were giggles. The second time was different, everyone gasped.

Harry had spotted the culprit. It was Col!

"Col, it's not funny! Cut it out."

Col is probably the naughtiest boy in our class, he is always in trouble with the teachers, has a weird sense of humor and tends to get into fights during the lunch breaks.

"Don't tell me what to do, Harry! I can blow some candles out if I want!" he said in an aggressive voice, pulling his shoulders back and staring at Harry.

Harry tried to calm the situation, "I'm just saying..."

Col put his hand into the cake and grabbed a huge hunk of it and threw it at Harry's face. Everyone was shocked! And then Harry quickly grabbed a handful of cake and threw it at Col. Gasps of horror escaped from the partygoers. And then Copy Cat Cate put her hand into the cake and threw some at Ivy. Ivy replied with a fistful of cake. This had turned into a full-on food fight! Cake was flying everywhere, some even hit Jordy's mother who was shouting for everyone to stop.

Sometimes it is handy being a witch. I put a freeze spell over everyone and reversed time, back to when we first surrounded the cake. I could see the precise moment Col was thinking about blowing out the candles. And at that precise second, I magically torpedoed a hot dog into his mouth. It flew up from the table and lodged itself firmly in his large ugly mouth.

Jordy blew out ALL his candles and we sang him Happy Birthday again.

Problem SOLVED!!!

I thought nobody had noticed, but straight after cutting of the cake, Lindy nudged me and gave me the thumbs up. "Good one, Sis," she whispered.

We all returned to the rink and skated until closing time. Hunky Harry hung around with me constantly. And as the announcement for the last song before closing was made, he whispered into my ear, "This has been the best day of my life."

Seriously, the BEST day??? What am I supposed to say to that???

"I've had a great day too, Hunk..." Wow, I just caught myself! "Harry," I quickly said.

He held my hands and stopped us from moving, looking into my eyes, he said, "Cindy, I know that you don't know me very well, but, I really like you. You are so different. And different in a good way."

Now he was rambling. What was he trying to say?

"Cindy, I was wondering if...you would be my girlfriend?" He smiled and looked a little shy.

And it was exactly then, that Poison Ivy crashed into us. She sent me flying through the air!

***

Did you enjoy Diary of an Almost Cool Witch?
Please let me know if you liked it!!!!

We would be extremely grateful if you could leave a review.
Thank you!!!!
Bill and Kaz

Some other books we think you will love...

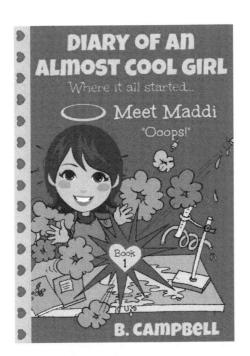

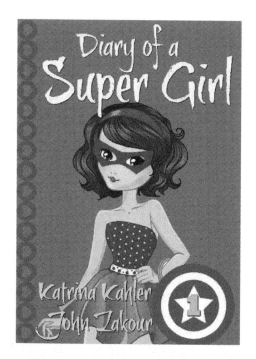

Made in the USA
San Bernardino, CA
23 December 2017